For Jackson

Copyright © 2015 by Marisabina Russo

All rights reserved. Published in the United States by Schwartz & Wade Books,

an imprint of Random House Children's Books, a division of Random House LLC, a Penguin Random House Company, New York.

Schwartz & Wade Books and the colophon are trademarks of Random House LLC.

Visit us on the Web! randomhousekids.com

Educators and librarians, for a variety of teaching tools, visit us at RHTeachersLibrarians.com

Library of Congress Cataloging-in-Publication Data

Russo, Marisabina, author, illustrator.

Little Bird takes a bath / Marisabina Russo. — First edition.

pages cm

Summary: The only thing Little Bird likes about rain is the puddles it leaves behind,

but after flying through Manhattan to find the perfect puddle, his bath is interrupted again and again.

ISBN 978-0-385-37014-1 (hc) — ISBN 978-0-385-37015-8 (glb) — ISBN 978-0-385-37016-5 (ebook)

[1. Birds—Fiction. 2. Rain and rainfall—Fiction. 3. Baths—Fiction.

4. City and town life—New York (State)—New York—Fiction. 5. New York (N.Y.)—Fiction.] I. Title.

PZ7.R9192Ljk 2015

[E]—dc23

2013018300

The text of this book is set in Berling.

The illustrations were rendered in gouache and colored pencil.

Book design by Rachael Cole

MANUFACTURED IN CHINA

2 4 6 8 10 9 7 5 3 1

First Edition

little bird takes a bath

Marisabina Russo

schwartz & wade books · new york

It was a rainy night in the city.

Little Bird sat looking at the street below.

He watched the umbrellas bobbing up and down.

He listened to the taxis honk-honk-honking.

He felt the thunder in his tiny wings.

"I don't like rain," said Little Bird.

"I don't like rain at all."

Then he nestled down

and closed his eyes

and dreamed about tomorrow.

In the morning Little Bird woke up early.

He looked out over the street below.

No more umbrellas, no more honking, no more thunder.

"Rain, rain, gone away," sang Little Bird,

who always started his day with a song.

"What a perfect day for a bath."

And off he flew—

over rooftops,

around lampposts,

under awnings.

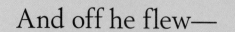

Little Bird saw puddles everywhere.

Some looked too big.

Some looked too small.

Some were already crowded with bathers.

At last Little Bird spotted the perfect puddle.

He swooped out of the sky

and landed with a happy splash.

"My puddle, my puddle, my puddle!" chirped Little Bird.

But then.

Something was

bounce

bounce

bouncing

straight at Little Bird. Oh, no!

He skittered out of the way.

When it was quiet again,

Little Bird hopped back into his puddle.

"That was close," he cheeped. "That was oh so close."

"Rub-a-dub-dub," sang Little Bird.

But then.

Something was

flip flop flapping

straight at Little Bird. Oh, no!

He flew out of the way faster than before.

When it was quiet again,

Little Bird hopped back into his puddle.

"That was closer," he cheeped. "That was even closer."

"Row, row, row your boat," sang Little Bird.

But then.

Something was

straight at Little Bird. Oh, no!

He flitted out of the way as fast as he could.

When it was quiet again,

Little Bird hopped back into his puddle.

"Closest yet!" he cheeped. "The very closest yet!"

But Little Bird wasn't happy with his puddle anymore.

Almost all the water had been splashed away.

Little Bird trilled a sad song:

"No more bath today. No more bath today."

Now he'd have to wait for another rainy night.

And remember? Little Bird didn't like rain.

He didn't like rain at all.

Little Bird flapped his tiny wings

and started to head home—

under awnings,

around lampposts,

over rooftops.

But then!

What was that, shining,

sparkling,

and shimmering

down below?

It looked like a fountain,

a splashy, swirly fountain,

just the right size for Little Bird.

Little Bird swooped out of the sky
and landed with a happy splash.
He shook and wiggled and fluttered his wings
until he was as clean as he could be.

At last Little Bird was ready to fly home.

He saw the long shadows spreading across the sidewalks.

He heard the loud buses rum-rum-rumbling down the streets.

He smelled the sweet aromas rising from the kitchen windows.

The sky was pink. There would be no rain tonight.

The moon's pale face appeared between two buildings

as Little Bird landed on his ledge.

"Good night, sweet sky, rock-a-bye," he sang,

because Little Bird always ended his day with a song.

Then he nestled down

and closed his eyes

and dreamed about tomorrow.